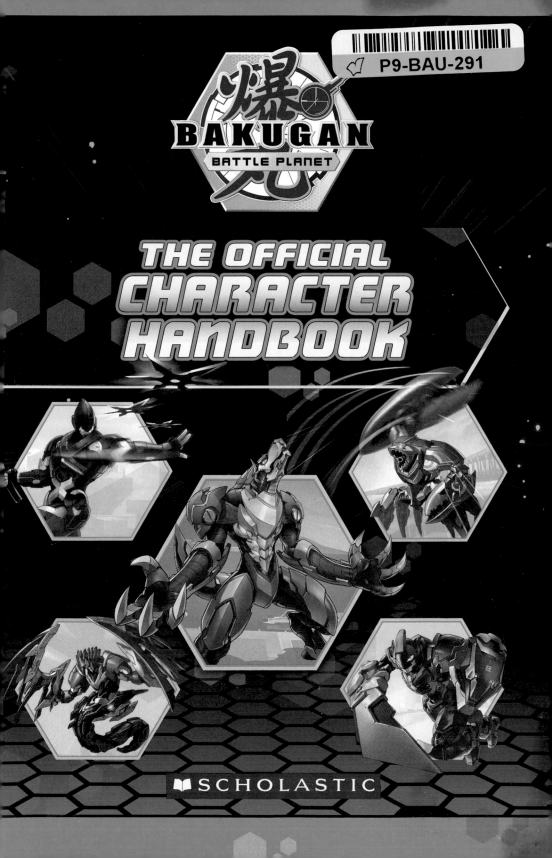

All rights reserved. Published by Scholastic Inc., *Publishers since 1920.* SCHOLASTIC and associated logos are trademarks and/or registered trademarks of Scholastic Inc.

The publisher does not have any control over and does not assume any responsibility for author or third-party websites or their content.

This book is a work of fiction. Names, characters, places, and incidents are either the product of the author's imagination or are used fictitiously, and any resemblance to actual persons, living or dead, business establishments, events, or locales is entirely coincidental.

ISBN 978-1-338-57490-6

10 9 8 7 6 5 4 3 2 1   20 21 22 23 24

Printed in the U.S.A.   40
First printing 2020

Designed by Jeff Shake

TABLE OF CONTENTS

WELCOME TO BAKUGAN: BATTLE PLANET!

A new age is dawning—the age of Bakugan. When these amazing alien creatures appeared on our planet, they could not remember where they came from. They partnered with humans they trusted. And with their humans, they honed their battle strategies and skills.

Almost as soon as the Bakugan appeared, evil forces sprang up—forces determined to control, enslave, or destroy these mysterious creatures. Leading the effort to protect the Bakugan—and the planet—is a group of kids who befriended the Bakugan.

Now it's up to Bakugan Brawlers everywhere to take up the fight—Brawlers just like you! In this handbook, you'll learn the story of Battle Planet, and how to spot the good guys and bad guys. You'll learn about the Bakugan and what they can do. And you'll learn how you can help the team uncover the secrets of a hidden world they call the Maze.

So what are you waiting for? Let's do this!

THE GREAT COLLISION

How did Bakugan enter our world?

It all began twelve years ago, on the night of the Great Collision. Strange clouds rolled across the sky above Pinpoint Park in the town of Los Volmos. Lightning crashed, and the sky opened up. Mysterious lights shot down, crashing into the ground below and creating a huge crater.

Something else happened that very night: a boy named Dan Kouzo was born. And on his twelfth birthday, he and his friends went to the site to make a video for the anniversary of the Great Collision. While they were there, their cell phones died. Lights appeared in the sky again, and they all heard an unusual word echoing around them: *Bakugan*.

Then, strange, swirling, white and blue goop bubbled up from the ground and flowed around their feet. Dan reached down to touch the glowing substance, and a small, red ball appeared in his hand.

Then a creature emerged, a majestic red dragon-like beast with massive wings.

"The name is Dragonoid," the creature said. "And I am your partner."

From that day forward, Dan helped bring Bakugan to the world . . . with the help of his friends.

AN AWESOME TEAM

The team started out as a group of friends—Dan Kouzo, Lia Venegas, Wynton Styles, and their dog, Lightning—who were famous for their funny videos on Linkster. But after that night, when Dan discovered the first Bakugan, Drago, everything changed. He and his friends became the team that introduced Bakugan to the world.

Lia, Wynton, and even Lightning quickly found Bakugan. They recorded themselves training with their Bakugan and battling each other. Kids around the world began to search for Bakugan and partner with them.

As the fame of their fame grew, some Brawlers wanted to join them. Only one was deemed worthy enough: Shun Kazami, who traveled all the way from Japan to join the team.

Dan, Wynton, Lia, Shun, and Lightning each bring different skills—and different Bakugan—to the team. Working together, they are the world's greatest hope for protecting Bakugan and solving the mystery of where they came from.

SOCIAL MEDIA STARS

Bakugan fans all over the world go to the team's channel on Linkster to view exciting battles, get tips on Bakugan training, and watch funny Bakugan videos and bloopers.

The videos usually start with an idea or vision by Lia, who directs and films them with her drone camera. Lightning is always a big hit; who doesn't love a cute dog, especially one who is an awesome Bakugan Brawler? Fans also tune in to watch Dan and Drago defeat their opponents in action-packed battles.

For a while, Wynton was popular for posting funny prank videos of his Bakugan, Trox. "Do not treat partnerships as a joke," Trox told Wynton. "Bakugan have feelings, too." But it wasn't until Trox deserted Wynton that he realized how much he was hurting his Bakugan. Wynton doesn't post prank videos of Trox anymore. Instead, he focuses on this dinosaur-like Bakugan's amazing battle skills.

BATTLE BASICS

"Drome up!"

When you hear someone shout those words, it means a Bakugan battle is about to begin. An enormous bubble—a Drome—will rise up, surrounding the Brawlers and anyone else who has a Bakugan that is with them. The drome keeps everyone outside the battle area safe. Whatever or whoever is inside the drome can receive damage. But the Drome provides protection from anything being permanently damaged. After the battle, the Drome disappears, and anything that was broken becomes fixed.

The basic rules of a Bakugan battle are pretty simple. Each Bakugan starts with a predetermined number of power points—this is their B Power. Trainers take turns instructing their Bakugan to launch a move against their opponent. Special abilities cause your opponent to lose points. Other kinds of moves can protect or heal your Bakugan. When one of the Bakugan's points drop to zero, the other Bakugan wins.

Inside the Drome is the Hide Matrix—a, floor made up of six-sided tiles called BakuCores. During a battle, some of these tiles light up. Brawlers can use the tiles to give their Bakugan more power points or to help them perform a special move by picking up the BakuCores and throwing them to their Bakugan.

The main purpose of Bakugan battles is for Brawlers and their partners to have fun and practice their skills. That's what it's supposed to be, anyway. There are evil forces out there who want to use Bakugan and their powers for their own gain Luckily, Dan and his friends are trying to stop them!

HAVING A BAKUGAN PARTNER

When a Bakugan enters our world, it chooses a human partner that it feels a connection with. A Bakugan will only choose a partner who was born after The Great Collision, which is why there are no adults who partner with Bakugan.

Having a Bakugan partner is just like having a friend. Bakugan partners work closely together, but they also listen to each other and respect each other. A human can give a Bakugan a command in battle, but there is no rule that the Bakugan has to follow it. If a Bakugan is not treated kindly by its partner, that Bakugan will end the partnership.

"Mutual trust and respect is essential between a Bakugan and its Brawler." —Lia

THE BAKUGAN CODE

A Bakugan Brawler should always have the best interests of Bakugan at heart. They all follow an unspoken code:

- Never ask your Bakugan to do anything bad.

- Never try to profit from your Bakugan.

- Never ask your Bakugan to do anything against its will.

- Always treat your Bakugan with kindness and respect.

*"Real Brawlers know one thing.
They know when Bakugan come first."* –Dan

FACTIONS INTRO

What's your battle style? Are you practiced and precise? A master manipulator? Bold and daring? Or something else?

Bakugan Brawlers have partners whose attacks and skills match their own battle styles. Each style, called a Faction, is represented by a different color and symbol. In this section, you'll read about the different Factions—and then take a quiz to find out which one you belong to!

AQUOS Color: Blue

If you need some help developing a battle strategy, ask an Aquos Brawler! They are focused and precise. Aquos players will often take their time deciding on their next move, waiting for the perfect moment to strike. A fast-moving Brawler, such as a Pyrus, can throw them off their game.

DARKUS Color: Black

Darkus Brawlers will use strategy to weaken your Bakugan, and then strike when you least expect it. Some of them are hungry for power, and will do whatever it takes to achieve the victory they crave. They are intense players who are very passionate about the game.

HAOS  Color: White

Haos Brawlers are most comfortable when they are in control of a battle. They work to get ahead of their opponents using strategies and BakuCores. To a Haos player, intelligent planning is more important than instinct.

PYRUS Color: Red

Pyrus players have lots of energy and battle with aggressive moves. They will strike first and ask questions later! Their strategy is to pummel their opponent with powerful attacks, and to win through quick damage.

VENTUS Color: Green

Ventus is the color of nature, and Ventus Brawlers will use their natural surroundings to gain an advantage during a battle. Green is also the color of growth, and Ventus Brawlers will train hard so that their skills can grow quickly.

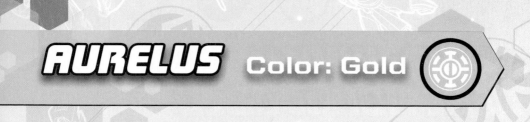

AURELUS Color: Gold

Not much is known about Aurelus Bakugan. Dan and his friends have encountered a mysterious golden bird Bakugan who appears to be helpful. And when they entered a strange dimension called the Maze, they battled a powerful Bakugan that also appeared to be an Aurelus. There's a good chance that the team will encounter more Aurelus Bakugan in the future.

QUIZ: WHICH FACTION WOULD YOU BELONG TO?

Circle your best answer to each question on the next page. Then use the key at the end to figure out what kind of Brawler you are: Aquos, Darkus, Haos, Pyrus, or Ventus.

1. **Pick an outdoor activity:**
   a. Gardening
   b. Swimming
   c. Camping
   d. Running
   e. Cave exploring

2. **Pick an ability to give your Bakugan:**
   a. Super strength
   b. Wave attack
   c. Fiery breath
   d. Flight
   e. Poison

3. **What word would your friends use to describe you?**
   a. Creative
   b. Calm
   c. Loud
   d. Smart
   e. Competitive

4. **What's the best terrain for a Bakugan battle?**
   a. A forest
   b. A sandy beach
   c. The base of a volcano
   d. On top of a mountain
   e. A large arena

5. **What's the best part of being a Bakugan Brawler?**
   a. It's fun!
   b. Figuring out new strategies
   c. Forging a bond with your Bakugan
   d. Making friends with other Brawlers
   e. Winning!

6. **What is your Brawling style?**
   a. Slow, then fast
   b. Careful
   c. Aggressive
   d. Defensive
   e. Determined

7. **What would your Brawler motto be?**
   a. Have fun and play hard!
   b. Make a plan and stick to it!
   c. Fight with all your might!
   d. Play fair and you'll never lose!
   e. Win at all costs!

8. **Which of these Bakugan is your favorite?**
   a. Trox
   b. Hydorous
   c. Dragonoid
   d. Pegatrix
   e. Nillious

9. **Pick a color.**
   a. Grass green
   b. Ocean blue
   c. Fire red
   d. Ice blue
   e. Midnight black

10. **Which of these Brawlers reminds you of yourself?**
    a. Wynton
    b. Shun
    c. Dan
    d. Lia
    e. Magnus

- **If you circled mostly a's:** You're a Ventus Brawler. Keep training, and don't be afraid to try out new moves when you're battling.

- **If you circled mostly b's:** You're an Aquos Brawler. Get comfortable making quick decisions so that unpredictable Brawlers don't throw you off your game.

- **If you circled mostly c's:** You're a Pyrus Brawler. Your powerful pummeling strategy usually works for you, but don't forget to learn defensive moves, too.

- **If you circled mostly d's:** You're a Haos Brawler. Other Brawlers could learn from your careful strategies, but don't forget to have fun when you play!

- **If you circled mostly e's:** You're a Darkus Brawler. You may win a lot, but your highly competitive nature may keep you from making friends with other Brawlers. Don't miss out on that—it's one of the best things about Bakugan!

THE HEROES AND THEIR BAKUGAN

When it comes to Bakugan, there are two types of Brawlers. Some respect their Bakugan and work to protect them; others try to exploit Bakugan for profit or power.

The Brawlers who fight the evil forces that use their Bakugan for personal gain are all heroes. Leading the charge are Dan Kouzo and his friends. In this section, you'll learn more about them—and their incredible Bakugan partners.

DAN KOUZO

"Let's do this!"

Faction:
Pyrus

Bakugan:
Dragonoid, Cyndeous

Dan's life has been connected to Bakugan since he was born: the day of The Great Collision. Twelve years later, on his birthday, he discovered Drago, the first Bakugan on Earth. Ever since then, he has been training and battling Bakugan, earning the reputation as the world's number one Brawler.

Bakugan players from all over seek out Dan and try to beat him. That's just fine with Dan—he loves a challenge! And while he doesn't think of himself as a leader, he is encouraging and supportive of other Brawlers. As a result, he has become the natural leader in the fight to protect Bakugan.

Dan rarely loses a battle, but when he does, he drowns his sorrows in a pile of cheeseburgers.

DRAGO

Partner:
Dan Kouzo

Noble. Powerful. Wise. Drago is all of these things, and more. A Pyrus Dragonoid, he only has vague memories of his life before The Great Collision. He has always felt a deep connection to other Bakugan, and he will do whatever it takes to protect his fellow creatures.

When Drago chose Dan to be his Bakugan partner, he chose wisely. Dan has a good heart, as well as a forceful battle style that perfectly matches Drago's powerful attacks. When Drago and Dan battle together, they're almost impossible to defeat!

Hyper Dragonoid

Drago connected to the energy of the Core Cell and evolved into Hyper Dragonoid, a ferocious, massive Bakugan. When the battle ended, Hyper Dragonoid became Drago once again.

CYNDEOUS

"Bakugan have feelings, too!"

Partner:
Dan Kouzo

This strong warrior Bakugan resembles a knight in armor. He is loyal to those he trusts, but he isn't afraid to play by his own rules, either.

Cyndeous first partnered with a boy named Marco, who turned out to be a bully. Marco challenged Dan to a duel and tried to order Cyndeous to attack Dan. "Human and Bakugan are friends," Cyndeous told Marco. "I will no longer fight this cowardly battle." He left Marco, and has been partnered with Dan ever since.

Cyndeous believes he's the best looking Bakugan around!

WYNTON STYLES

"We grow stronger every day!"

Faction:
Ventus

Bakugan:
Trox, Lupitheon, Turtonium

Wynton's a prankster, a tech head, and an amazing Brawler. Even though he jokes around a lot, he cares deeply for his Bakugan and his friends. Some might say he's a slacker-hacker, and that's true, but his inventive solutions often save the day when his friends are in trouble.

When Wynton's not training, battling, or inventing something, he likes to play pranks. Most of them get a lot of hits on the team's Linkster channel. On his own birthday, he surprised Lia with a pie in the face. He likes to surprise others, but doesn't like it when it happens to him!

Wynton and Dan have been friends since the second grade. They met when Dan broke his handheld game system, and Wynton fixed it with a paper clip and some gum.

TROX

Partner:
Wynton Styles

He might look like a raging dinosaur, but Trox is usually thoughtful and strategic in battle. If he starts to lose or is in pain, though, he becomes a rampaging beast. Trox and Wynton train hard, and in battle they work together like a well-oiled machine.

Hyper Trox

Bigger, fiercer, sharper—Trox becomes all of these things when he evolves into Hyper Trox.

LUPITHEON

Partner:
Wynton Styles

What's that howl? It must be Lupitheon, a werewolf-like Bakugan. His sharp claws and teeth strike fear into the hearts of his opponents. Like other werewolves, he becomes even stronger when the full moon is out.

Lupitheon appeared to Wynton on the Brawler's birthday. The two got to know each other quickly when Col. Tripp gained control of Drago and Trox. Lupitheon joined Dan's Bakugan, Cyndeous, in a ferocious battle. Under the light of a full moon, Lupitheon gained enough power to save the night.

TURTONIUM

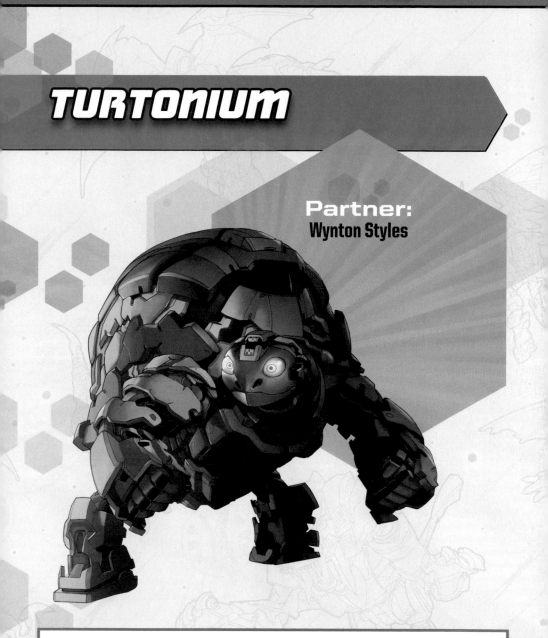

Partner:
Wynton Styles

This tortoise-like Bakugan is patient and wise. An excellent strategist, he helps Wynton plan attacks. He's not much of a fighter; instead, he uses his powers to heal Trox, and other Bakugan Lupitheon during battles.

LIA VENEGAS

"Bakugan, brawl!"

Faction:
Haos

Bakugan:
Pegatrix, Gorthion, Cubbo

Lia's artistic eye helped catapult the team to Linkster superstardom. She brings her creativity to the Bakugan battlefield, where she combines her instincts and skill to cast all the right moves.

Lia has no patience for bullies and haters. She'll quickly put them in their place, and when she sees someone who needs help, she jumps right in.

Lia's mom is a TV news reporter, which might be why Lia is so good with a camera.

PEGATRIX

Partner:
Lia Venegas

"Overwhelming an opponent with power isn't a beautiful strategy," Pegatrix told Lia the first time they battled together. This Bakugan does have some powerful attacks, but she prefers healing her teammates over using brute force.

Pegatrix appeared to Lia inside a white flower. She chose a human partner with a good heart, but she doesn't always agree with Lia's actions—and is sure to tell her so.

Hyper Pegatrix

In her evolved form, Pegatrix becomes a majestic steed with lightning speed and massive wings.

GORTHION

Partner:
Lia Venegas

"Am I going bananas?"

In the heat of battle, this huge, gorilla-like Bakugan will let out a mighty roar and lash out in fury at his opponents. Cool-headed Lia is the perfect partner for this hot-tempered Bakugan. She can calm him down and guide him to victory.

He might look fierce, but a kind heart beats inside that massive chest. He will throw himself in harm's way in the blink of an eye to protect Lia.

CUBBO

Partner:
Lia Venegas

This tiny, teddy bear–like Bakugan might look cute, but he's actually a trash-talking little tough guy. After she and her friends returned from the Maze, Lia found Cubbo's Bakugan ball in her hair. Cubbo didn't want to partner with anybody—but Lia showered him with unconditional love, and cracked his hard shell. He agreed to be her partner.

Cubbo and Lia both share a wicked sense of humor. They quickly bonded by watching bloopers of their videos—especially the ones involving Dan and Wynton!

SHUN KAZAMI

"For my friends, for my Bakugan, and for myself, I will fight!"

Faction:
Aquos

Bakugan:
Hydorous, Fade Ninja, Vicerox

Shun Kazami traveled all the way from Japan to Los Volmos to try out for the team. At first, Dan didn't know what to make of this serious boy dressed in a crisp blue suit. But Shun quickly impressed everyone—not just with his battle skills, but because he understood the importance of working with a team.

Mature and mysterious on the outside, Shun has a passion for Bakugan that burns on the inside. When his father ordered him to come back to Japan, Shun battled Col. Tripp to show his dad just what he and his Bakugan could accomplish together.

Shun lived alone when he first came to Los Volmos, but now he lives with Wynton and his family.

Partner:
Shun Kazami

Hydorous resembles a lion, with sharp claws, sharp fangs, and an intimidating roar. He has cat-like agility on the battlefield.

While Shun is quiet and calm, Hydorous is aggressive and fierce. Even though they are opposites, their styles work well together in battle. Hydorous helps fuel Shun's competitive nature, and Shun helps Hydorous use his moves more effectively.

Hydorous enjoys playing video games with Wynton's little brother.

Hyper Hydorous

Sharper, stronger, faster—Hydorous becomes a more powerful version of himself when he evolves.

FADE NINJA

Partner:
Shun Kazami

Tall, muscled, and armored, this Bakugan looks like a human warrior. Fade Ninja boasts some impressive battle moves, including Clone Army. When he uses it, dozens of copies of Fade Ninja appear on the battlefield.

Fade Ninja wasn't always partnered with Shun. He was used by Toshi, the bodyguard to Shun's father. Toshi came to Los Volmos to bring Shun back to Japan, and Shun challenged him to a battle. Hydorous defeated Fade Ninja, and Toshi was so impressed with Shun's battling style that he gave him Fade Ninja as a gift.

VICEROX

Partner:
Shun Kazami

As it scuttles across the battlefield on its claws, you might think this Bakugan looks like a giant crab. Then you'll be amazed as it unleashes controlled, powerful attacks.

Shun was also given Vicerox by Toshi, his father's bodyguard. The evil Col. Tripp challenged Shun to a battle so he could win Hydorous from him. Toshi gave Shun Vicerox to help even up the sides, and Shun prevailed.

LIGHTNING

Faction:
Darkus

Bakugan:
Howlkor,
Artulean,
Phaedrus

When Dan discovered this cute stray bulldog near his home, he quickly became the mascot for the team. After all, everyone knows that cute dog videos get millions of hits on social media, right?

But after Dan and his friends discovered Bakugan, something amazing happened. Lightning partnered with a Bakugan, too—Howlkor. Then he met another Bakugan—Artulean. Wynton created a special collar for Lightning so that he can carry his Bakugan with him wherever he goes.

Now he's more than a mascot—he's a valuable member of the team. Lightning is small, so he can get into places that the others can't. And when trouble arises, he snaps into battle mode and brawls with his teammates. Sure, he might need a nap and a treat afterwards—but so does Dan!

Lightning can't talk. Just like other dogs, he communicates with barks, growls, and body language.

HOWLKOR

Partner:
Lightning

"Lightning, put me in!"

Why would a ferocious dog with three heads choose an adorable French bulldog to be his Bakugan partner? Howlkor was attracted to Lightning's animal nature, figuring that another dog would understand him.

Lightning is actually a little afraid of his Bakugan. He'll have to learn to be the alpha dog if he ever wants to get Howlkor under control. In the meantime, though, Lightning doesn't hesitate to use Howlkor when his friends are in trouble!

Hyper Howlkor

Lightning evolved Howlkor during a battle with Strata the Hunter. Hyper Howlkor is even more terrifying than his original form!

ARTULEAN

Partner:
Lightning

"I'm Artulean. Pleased to make your acquaintance!"

Artulean resembles a noble knight with a powerful laser cannon on each shoulder. Even though he's mighty, he's always polite and tries to do the right thing.

Artulean chose Lightning as his partner one day in the park. Immediately, Howlkor challenged him to battle. That started a rivalry between the two Bakugan: Artulean then pranked Howlkor, and Howlkor got annoyed. But the two proved that they could work together when Magnus threatened their friends.

KEY BRAWLS

Dan and his friends have had their skills tested in many Brawls. Here are some that they'll never forget.

Dan vs. Magnus

Magnus had challenged Dan and Drago again and again—and always lost. But one memorable day, Magnus showed up with renewed determination and a strange device on his arm. During the battle, Dan watched, amazed, as Magnus used the device to evolve Nillious into a newer, stronger, form! Nillious decimated Drago, and Magnus finally defeated Dan. This loss left Dan wondering how Magnus got the strange device—and a surprise visit from Magnus's little sister Emily hinted that Magnus was a pawn in a sinister game.

Trox vs. Drago, Cyndeous, and Gorthion

When Wynton and Trox argued over Wynton's prank videos, they made a deal: if Trox beat Drago, Cyndeous, and Gorthion in a battle, he could leave Wynton and find a new partner. Nobody thought Trox could win in a three-in-one battle, but Trox was confident. He had seen all of his friends' moves many times, and knew exactly how to avoid receiving damage.

When Trox's three opponents hit him with their best attacks, Trox used Rock Riser to make a huge hole in the ground. While he hid, his foes hit each other with their attacks and lost all their points!

Trox may have won, but after Wynton apologized, he agreed to remain his partner.

Shun vs. Masato

When his cousin Masato came to bring Shun back to Japan, Shun was in shock. Torn by his dedication to the team and to his family, he didn't fight back when Masato attacked with his Serpenteze.

But when Shun decided that staying with his new friends was the right thing to do, he battled Masato with all of his might. During the battle, he forged a strong connection with Hydorous, which caused his Bakugan to evolve. Hyper Hydorous broke through Serpenteze's defense and finished him with a barrage of Aquos attacks.

The Whole Team vs. Strata the Hunter

When a Bakugan named Phaedrus told the team that Bakugan were being captured, they agreed to help. She led them to a mansion in the mysterious place known as the Maze. There they found Strata the Hunter, who was holding the captured Bakugan.

The team brought out Drago, Gorthion, and Trox to battle Strata and his Krakelios. But battling in the Maze was nothing like battling on Earth. Krakelios kept attacking and then hiding in the Maze. Finally, Lightning sniffed out Krakelios, and Phaedrus took down the Aquos Bakugan with a powerful thunderbolt attack.

That gave Phaedrus and Lightning the chance to free the captured Bakugan. But Strata and Krakelios attacked with Aquos Flash, sending the team and their Bakugan falling deep into the Maze . . .

THE VILLAINS AND THEIR BAKUGAN

It happened so fast—as soon as kids discovered Bakugan, adults searched for ways to use Bakugan for their own gain. Because these villains were born before The Great Collision, they had to find other, sinister ways to control them.

Some villains work on their own, hunting for powerful Bakugan. Others work for corporations looking to make money from Bakugan. And the motives of some others remain a mystery. In this section, you'll meet them all.

MAGNUS BLACK

"I will crush them!"

Faction:
Darkus

Bakugan:
Nillious, Fangzor, Webam

Dan first met Magnus when the mysterious masked boy challenged him to a Brawl on the street. Up until that point, Dan had been battling other Brawlers for fun. But Magnus and his Darkus Nillious seemed deathly serious. "This could change the fate of the world," Magnus told Dan.

What Dan didn't know was that Magnus had agreed to work for AAAnimus Inc., a shady corporation run by Philomena Dusk. Magnus doesn't know why Philomena is obsessed with defeating Dan Kouzo, and he doesn't care. He's doing it because she has the technology to help his sick sister, Emily.

While Magnus might be Brawling for noble reasons, his jealousy of Dan has turned his heart cold and dark. Emily says that Magnus is really good inside, but time will tell if that is still true.

NILLIOUS

Partner:
Magnus Black

Does the fact that this Bakugan has two heads mean it is twice as dangerous as other Bakugan? Maybe not, but it does double Nillious's desire to destroy his opponents. Unlike other Bakugan, he doesn't care about winning—only about how much damage he can cause.

Nillious only barely tolerates having Magnus as a partner, and likes to go rogue. This means Magnus has to work hard to keep his Bakugan in line—and the fact that each head has a different personality only makes it harder.

Hyper Nillious

When Nillious evolves, he becomes bigger, stronger, and much harder to damage.

FANGZOR

Partner:
Magnus Black

The most dangerous feature of this snake-like Bakugan is his sharp fangs, which can inject deadly poison into his opponents. This sneaky snake is a favorite Bakugan of many villains, but Magnus's Darkus Fangzor might be the creepiest one of all.

WEBAM

Partner:
Magnus Black

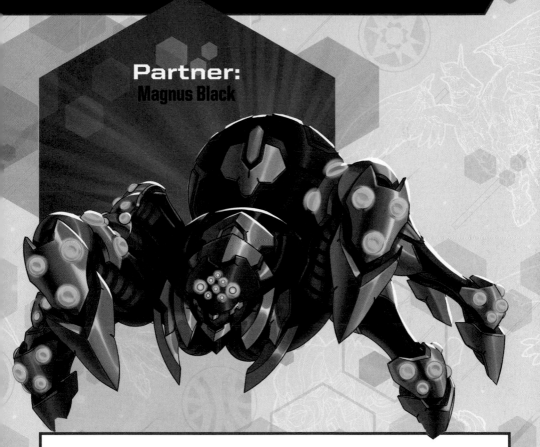

What has eight legs and loves to battle? Webam! This Bakugan looks like an enormous tarantula, and fits right in with Magnus's stable of spooky creatures.

STRATA THE HUNTER

"Now your Bakugan can join my little collection!"

Faction:
Aquos

Bakugan:
Krakelios

Strata used to hunt wild game all over the world. When he heard about Bakugan, he developed a new mission: to use his hunting techniques to track down and capture Bakugan. When he succeeds, he drains their energy with a special weapon he invented, leaving them as lifeless as statues. Then he displays them as trophies in his mansion.

Strata is one of the most despicable villains Dan and his friends have encountered; he treats Bakugan like objects to collect and dominate, not as the majestic creatures with feelings that they are.

KRAKELIOS

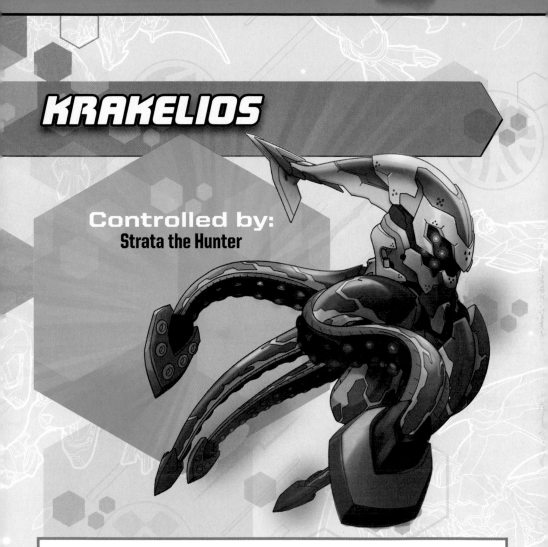

Controlled by:
Strata the Hunter

This Bakugan resembles a mighty sea serpent and is just as frightening as anything you might read about in legends. Krakelios has an advantage in water and can silently sneak up on an opponent, surrounding them with all eight of its legs. When Strata uses Krakelios inside the Maze, it can disappear and reappear to make surprise attacks.

Tip:

If you want to take down Krakelios, try attacking from the sky.

CHINA RIOT

"Please don't be a meanie to my Maxotaur!"

Faction:
Ventus

Bakugan:
Maxotaur

This spoiled six-year-old girl may be cute, but there's nothing cute about her battle skills. She's as brave as they come and has a will as strong as her tough Bakugan, Maxotaur Ultra.

When China challenges another Brawler, it's not for kicks—it's for cash. She's been hired by AAAnimus Inc. She's happy to battle to keep up her lavish lifestyle, which includes a personal butler and a private helicopter.

MAXOTAUR

Partner:
China Riot

Part monster, part dinosaur: No matter what Maxotaur looks like to you, the important thing to know is that he's a powerful, wild beast. He doesn't say much during battle, but he doesn't have to. His mighty fists and sharp sword do the talking for him.

This big brute is happy to take orders from China. In a battle, he'd rather be told what to do than to have to think or strategize.

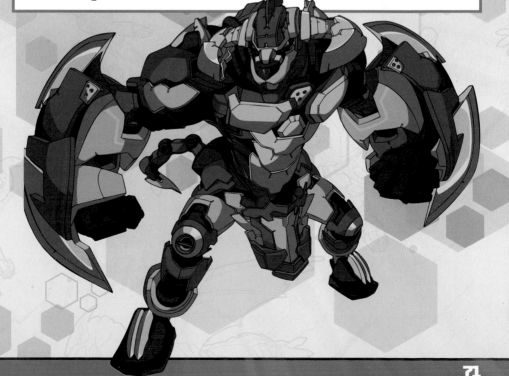

MARCO CHEZANELLO

He might not be as sinister as the other villains, but Marco has caused plenty of trouble for Dan and his friends. It started when he took over Pinpoint Park and wouldn't let other Brawlers play there. He defended the park with his Bakugan, Cyndeous.

"You have to do whatever I say, like it or not," Marco told Cyndeous. But Marco had betrayed his partnership with the Bakugan. Partners don't order each other around—they work together to create strategies. Cyndeous left Marco that day to become Dan's partner.

DURAN DANE

"Don't tell me what to do!"

Dan and Wynton first met Duran when they thought they had been hired to teach him how to train Bakugan. Duran challenged them to a battle with his Bakugan, Nobilious. The battle took place in a mysterious underground cavern where the rules of the game had completely changed. The battle ended when Nobilous confided to Drago that he didn't want to obey Duran, but he had to. He let Dan, Wynton, and their Bakugan escape.

Later, Dan and Wynton met Duran again. He confessed that he was an actor who had been hired to battle them the first time by their friend, Benton Dusk. Duran battled them again—this time, for fame. But he only proved that he's a better actor than he is a Brawler.

Nobilious is an enormous Bakugan that resembles a griffin, a mythological creature that is half-eagle, half-lion.

PHILOMENA DUSK

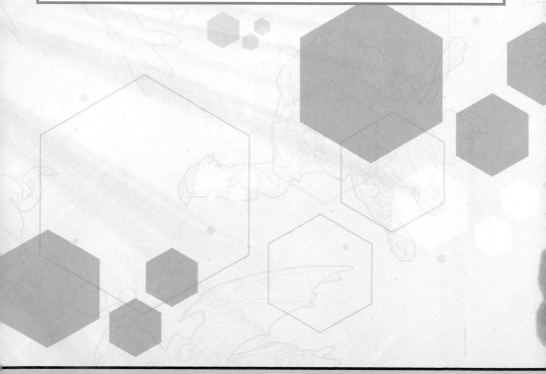

The head of AAAnimus Inc. has spent a fortune trying to defeat Dan and his friends: but why? They aren't quite sure, but they are learning more about this flashy villain.

According to her younger brother, Benton Dusk, Philomena has been collecting data on the heroes to further her research into the Bakugan phenomenon. She has a team of scientists working to unlock the secrets of Bakugan, which she hopes to profit from.

She's mean, she's smart, and she's ruthless. The Bakugan evolution device she had implanted on Magnus's arm pushed the boy to the limits of his endurance—but Philomena didn't care. When she wants results, she'll do anything to get them, no matter what the cost.

THE EXIT TEAM

This team of kid Brawlers might have been Philomena's most brilliant idea. At first, they were carefully selected for their style and personality to create Bakugan videos that would become more popular online than Dan and his friends. But the Exit Team couldn't defeat the heroes.

The team may have failed, but Philomena kept the concept. She re-formed the Exit Team with villains who had already proven themselves against in battle: Magnus, China Riot, Strata the Hunter, Aay (the leader of the first Exit), and Kurin, a cheating Brawler who had secretly taped Dan and his friends so he could learn their battle moves.

The upgraded Exit Team succeeded where the first team failed. They staged disasters and then recorded themselves saving the day. They quickly became heroes, and made the Dan's team look like bad guys!

Green and Mean

Dan and his friends encountered the first leader of the exit, Aay, several times. The first time, he was using his Bakugan, Mantonoid, to rob Dan's favorite burger joint.

COL. ARMSTRONG TRIPP

"Deploy Pandoxx Punch!"

Faction:
Haos

Bakugan:
Pandoxx

He may look like a military man, but Col. Tripp doesn't answer to the government: he answers to Philomena Dusk. He's the number-one adult Bakugan Brawler and leads a team of other adults enhanced by AAAnimus Inc. technology to become better Brawlers.

Tripp is armed with some of the most sinister technology AAAnimus has developed: a device that latches onto a Bakugan and allows Tripp to control it. He even used the device to control Wynton!

PANDOXX

Controlled by:
Col. Tripp

On its own, this panda-like Bakugan delivers its powerful attacks with honor, in the spirit of Bakugan competition. But when controlled by the evil Col. Tripp, this Pandoxx becomes a ruthless, punishing beast.

Dan and his friendsfirst encountered Pandoxx when they were sent a video of the Bakugan being captured. They traveled into the woods to find it, only to learn they had fallen into a trap by Tripp. They tried to save Pandoxx, but could not free it from Tripp's control.

MASATO KAZAMI

"Shun, you are a helpful research subject."

Shun's older cousin, Masato, works for Shun's father in the Kazami International Holdings. Mr. Kazami let Shun live in Los Volmos with his new friends for a while, but then decided he wanted his son back—to extract all the research Shun learned about Bakugan and the Core Cell. He sent Masato to bring Shun back.

Masato is cold and calculating. He does what he is told without emotion, for the good of Kazami Holdings. To him, obeying the family is more important than whether what he is being asked to do is right or wrong.

SERPENTEZE

Controlled by:
Masato Kazami

Serpenteze is no ordinary snake. This Bakugan has a serpent's body, as well as large wings. In battle, Serpenteze can be silent and sneaky.

Masato loves to be in control, but Serpenteze is unpredictable and often disobeys his Brawler. Masato doesn't mind, because sometimes this Bakugan's surprise attacks are more effective than anything he could plan himself.

A NEW DIMENSION

One by one, challengers faced Dan and his team. And one by one, Dan, Lia, Wynton, Shun, and Lightning defeated them.

But then the game changed. The friends found themselves in a strange new place. There, they faced new challenges and a mysterious Bakugan more dangerous than any they had ever seen before.

With the fate of all Bakugan in the balance, they battled like they never had before. Their own fate was in the balance, too: it looked like they might be trapped in this new dimension forever . . .

BENTON DUSK

"I have been researching Bakugan for a long time."

Benton, the brother of Philomena Dusk, is a wealthy genius who has been studying Bakugan ever since they first appeared. When the team met him, he told them that his mission was to protect Bakugan from people who want to exploit them, like his sister. But why is he so focused on linking all the Core Cells together? And why is he so interested in the Maze?

Dan and his friends began to doubt Benton after Duran Dane told them that it was Benton who hired him to battle Dan and Wynton. Can Benton still be trusted, or is Duran lying to them? The heroes aren't sure, but one thing is certain: it was Benton who first introduced them to the mysterious dimension known as the Maze.

PHAEDRUS

When Strata the Hunter captured Bakugan and kept them in a prison in the Maze, Phaedrus escaped through a portal. This dragon-like Bakugan emerged in the headquarters of Benton Dusk and asked for his help, and Benton called on Dan and his team.

Phaedrus doesn't Brawl with Benton, but she found a new home with him once she helped the team free her captured friends. Eventually, Phaedrus decides to team up with Lightning instead.

THE MAZE